## A NOTE TO PARENTS

When your children are ready to "step into reading," giving them the right books is as crucial as giving them the right food to eat. **Step into Reading Books** present exciting stories and information reinforced with lively, colorful illustrations that make learning to read fun, satisfying, and worthwhile. They are priced so that acquiring an entire library of them is affordable. And they are beginning readers with a difference—they're written on five levels.

**Early Step into Reading Books** are designed for brand-new readers, with large type and only one or two lines of very simple text per page. **Step 1 Books** feature the same easy-to-read type as the Early Step into Reading Books, but with more words per page. **Step 2 Books** are both longer and slightly more difficult, while **Step 3 Books** introduce readers to paragraphs and fully developed plot lines. **Step 4 Books** offer exciting nonfiction for the increasingly independent reader.

The grade levels assigned to the five steps—preschool through kindergarten for the Early Books, preschool through grade 1 for Step 1, grades 1 through 3 for Step 2, grades 2 through 3 for Step 3, and grades 2 through 4 for Step 4—are intended only as guides. Some children move through all five steps very rapidly; others climb the steps over a period of several years. Either way, these books will help your child "step into reading" in style!

Published in the United States by Random House, Inc., New York, and simultaneously in Canada by Random House of Canada Limited, Toronto.

CRITTERS OF THE NIGHT® and all prominent characters featured in this book and the distinctive likenesses thereof are trademarks of Big Tuna Trading Company, LLC.

www.randomhouse.com/kids/

*Library of Congress Cataloging-in-Publication Data*
Farber, Erica.
Zoom on my broom / written by Erica Farber and J. R. Sansevere.
    p. cm. — (Step into reading. A step 1 book) (Mercer Mayer's critters of the night)
SUMMARY: A visit to Thistle Howl's house includes a snack of green cheese and rice and bug juice on ice and a zoom around the room on her broom.
ISBN 0-679-88710-5 (trade) — ISBN 0-679-98710-X (lib. bdg.)
[1. Monsters—Fiction. 2. Stories in rhyme.]
I. Sansevere, J.R. II. Title. III. Series: Step into reading. Step 1 book. IV. Series: Critters of the night.
PZ8.3.F2167Zo 1998
[E]—dc21 98-16811

**Printed in Mexico**        10  9  8  7  6  5  4  3  2  1
STEP INTO READING is a registered trademark of Random House, Inc.

A BIG TUNA TRADING COMPANY, LLC/J. R. SANSEVERE BOOK

Step into Reading®

# MERCER MAYER'S
# CRITTERS OF THE NIGHT®
# ZOOM ON MY BROOM

Written by
Erica Farber and J. R. Sansevere

**A Step 1 Book**

Random House 🏠 New York

Hello! Hello!

Please come with me.

There's lots to do.

And lots to see.

# This is my cat.

# Let's take a ride.

7

I like to ride

my cat inside.

This is our cook.

He likes to bake.

He bakes a cake

for our pet snake.

This is my dad.

This is Dad's hat.

Out of his hat,

Dad pulls a bat.

This is my pot.

Let's make a brew.

One cup for me.

One cup for you.

# Where is my mom?

Here she is now!

# Poof goes her wand.

# Look at the cow!

One cow,

now two.

Three cows,

now four.

Poof goes Mom's wand.

Here come some more!

# This is my tub.

# That is my fish.

You can pet him

if you wish!

Let's have a snack.

Green cheese and rice.

Two scoops of goop.

Bug juice on ice.

This is my room.

# That is my broom.

# Zoom on my broom

# around the room!

It's time to go.

I wave good-bye!

We had such fun,

my friend and I.